New Clues About DINOSAURS

Contents

Rigby

If you want to learn about an elephant, you can go to a zoo and study it. If you want to learn about a dinosaur, you have to be a better detective. You can only study the clues in the fossils that dinosaurs left behind.

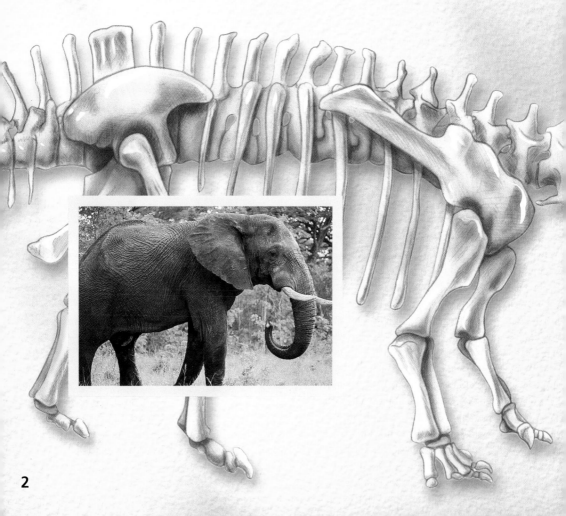

Three Steps to Studying Fossils:

DISCOVERY

finding the fossils

OBSERVATION

gathering and sorting information

THEORY

making a guess about what the fossils tell us about dinosaur life

Scientists have been studying dinosaur fossils for more than 175 years. In that time, new discoveries and new technology have led to new theories, or ideas, about dinosaurs.

Then

In the 1800s, scientists began to discover many dinosaur fossils. They used scales and microscopes to make detailed observations. They came up with theories about dinosaurs by using this information and their imaginations.

Now

Scientists study fossils from old and new digs. They make more exact observations with scanning machines and computers. This new information sometimes makes scientists change old ideas.

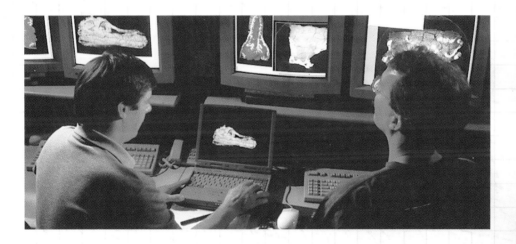

But they still use their imaginations, along with their computers. Let's take a look at some old theories about dinosaurs, and how they are changing.

Looking at Horns

1824 England

DISCOVERY

A few teeth and a horn are discovered.

OBSERVATION

Teeth look like an iguana's, but are
20 times larger.

Horn is like
a rhinoceros's.

OLD THEORY

These fossils belonged to a giant reptile
that had a horn on its nose.

1857 England

DISCOVERY

A more complete skeleton of Iguanadon, including two horns, is found.

OBSERVATION

The horns fit on the leg bones.

NEW THEORY

Iguanadon had thumb spikes on its front legs, but no horn on its nose.

Looking at Crests

1923 Canada

A Hadrosaur skull with a crest is found.

The weight of the long, narrow crest shows it must have been hollow.

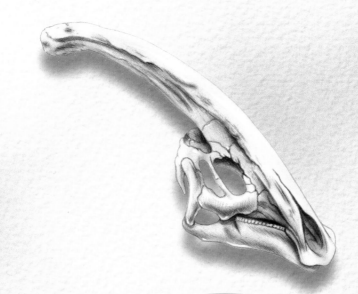

The crest held air.

1995 USA

A complete Hadrosaur skull is found.

Computer scans show the inside of the crest.
The crest holds tubes like those
in musical instruments.

Gerrity

The crest helped Hadrosaur make
different sounds.

Looking at Tails

1877 USA

Skeleton of Apatosaurus is discovered.

The neck and tail both measure
more than 40 feet.

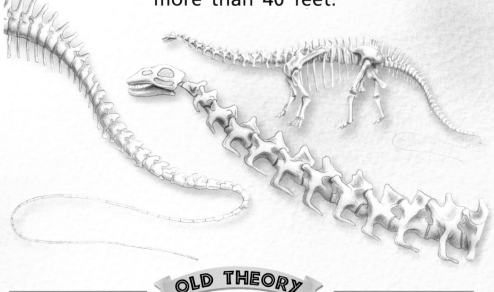

OLD THEORY

The tail was dragged on the ground to balance
the weight of the neck and head. It might
have been used as a whip.

1993 USA

Apatosaurus skeleton is copied
as a computer model.

OBSERVATION

Computer animation shows the tail was carried
higher and did have a structure like a whip.

NEW THEORY

Apatosaurus could have cracked its tail like
a whip making a loud, cannon-like boom.

11

Looking at Necks

1877 USA

DISCOVERY

Parts of a Diplodocus skeleton are discovered.

OBSERVATION

The long neck of this herbivore could have reached the tops of the trees.

OLD THEORY

Diplodocus reached up to the tops of trees to eat leaves.

1995 USA

DISCOVERY

Diplodocus skeleton is copied
as a computer model.

OBSERVATION

Computer animation shows the neck bones
could raise the head only to shoulder height.

NEW THEORY

Diplodocus only ate low-growing plants.

Looking at Skin

1908 USA

DISCOVERY

An almost complete Trachodon skin is found.

OBSERVATION

Skin fossils show texture, but not color. The skin of dinosaurs was scaly and tough, like the skin of living reptiles.

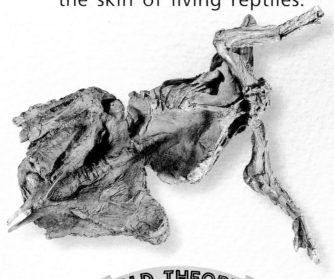

OLD THEORY

Dinosaurs were the same color as lizards and crocodiles.

1997 Australia

Microscopic color cells are discovered
in fossils of ancient fish.

OBSERVATION

Ancient cells can be matched with those
of modern fish, to find which color
each cell made.

NEW THEORY

Some color cells of modern fish match cells in
dinosaur skin fossils. This will help us to know
the colors of dinosaurs!

Looking at Eggs

1923 China

DISCOVERY

Skeleton of a small carnivore is found.

OBSERVATION

The skeleton was found crouching over
a nest of eggs.

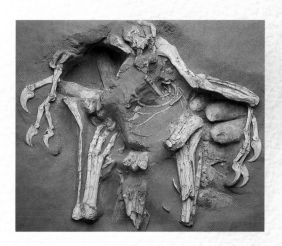

OLD THEORY

This dinosaur took eggs from
nests for its dinner. The dinosaur's name,
Oviraptor, means "egg thief."

1993 China

DISCOVERY

More eggs from the same nest are studied.

OBSERVATION

This egg had the skeleton of a
baby Oviraptor inside.

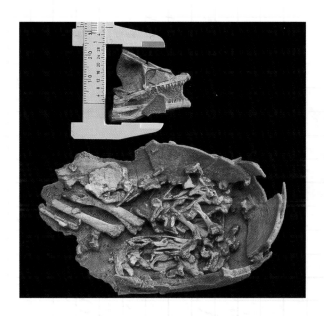

NEW THEORY

The small dinosaur was crouching over her
own nest! Oviraptor needs a new name.

Looking at Nests

1978 USA

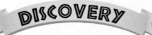

Nests with skeletons in and around them are discovered in a group.

Nests were carefully made.

Some dinosaurs, like Titanosaurus, lived in groups and cared for their babies.

1990 Argentina

Thousands of nests with many eggs are found.

Nests are stacked on top of each
other for 15 feet.

NEW THEORY

Titanosaurus not only lived in
large groups but used the same nesting
place year after year.

Discovery Time Line

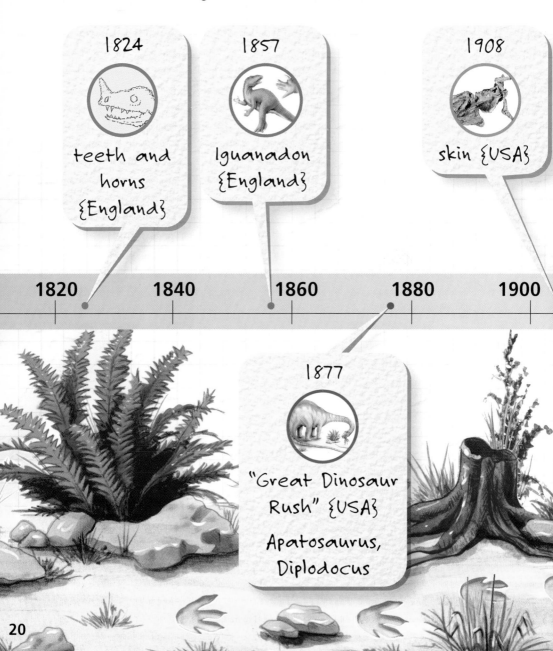

1824
teeth and horns {England}

1857
Iguanadon {England}

1908
skin {USA}

1820   1840   1860   1880   1900

1877
"Great Dinosaur Rush" {USA}
Apatosaurus, Diplodocus

1978

nests {USA}

1990

nests and
bones
{Argentina}

1993

eggs {China}
computer
animation
done {USA}

1920	1940	1960	1980	2000

1923

eggs and
nests
{China}
Hadrosaur
crest
{Canada}

1995

computer
scans of
Hadrosaur
crests {USA}

1997

color cells
in fish
{Australia}

2000 and Beyond

New species of dinosaurs are still being discovered. New technologies help scientists learn more from fossils. New theories add to our knowledge of these animals. New questions excite our imaginations.

What will be the next dinosaur discovery?

Index